FREE WILLY 2

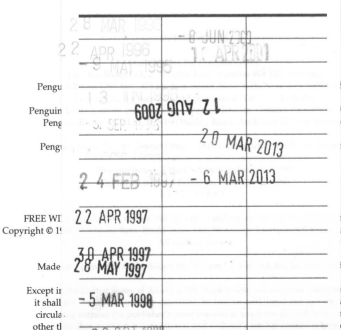

Adapted by Nancy E. Krulik
Based on the Motion Picture
Written by Karen Janszen and Corey Blechman and John Mattson
Based on Characters Created by Keith A. Walker

Pengu... USA

Penguin... 3B2
Peng...

Pengu... d

"Willy! Willy!"

Jesse screamed the whale's name as loud as he could. It had been two years since Jesse and his friend Randolph rescued the orca from his tank in an amusement park. Together they'd set him free. Back then, Jesse was sure he would never see Willy again. But now, here he was, watching Willy swim with his family.

Seeing Willy again almost made up for the fact that Jesse had to share his holiday with his long-lost half-brother, Elvis.

Jesse had been planning this holiday with his foster parents, Glen and Annie, for a long time. They were going whale watching with Randolph. Everything was all set when, all of a sudden, Elvis arrived at Glen and Annie's house. Up until then, Jesse didn't even know he *had* a half-brother. Now he found himself sharing a tent with him. Worse still, Jesse had a strange feeling that Annie was going to ask Elvis to move in with them – the same way she'd taken Jesse in two years ago.

3

That night, after Annie and Elvis had gone to their tents, Jesse and Glen sat and watched the campfire burn.

"Do you think Willy misses me?" Jesse asked Glen.

"Jesse, when you're in someone's heart, you stay there for ever," Glen said kindly. "Besides, you have your family, too. Just like Willy."

Jesse hoped that by the time he got back to his tent, Elvis would be fast asleep. But Elvis was not a great sleeper. He was wide awake and ready to talk.

Elvis was a real show-off – and a liar. The boy was really starting to bug Jesse. Jesse drew a pretend line down the middle of the tent. "See this line?" he asked. "Don't even think about crossing it."

Elvis just laughed and put his foot on Jesse's side of the tent.

Enough was enough! Jesse bolted out of the tent and down to the dock.

Jesse sat alone and looked out across the water. He took his harmonica out of his pocket and began to play a sad tune. But the harmonica slipped out of his hand.

Whoosh! A wave of water splashed on to the jetty. Jesse was soaked to the skin. It was Willy! He had Jesse's harmonica in his mouth. He had heard Jesse playing. And just like the old days, he'd raced straight over.

"I've missed you, old boy," Jesse said, stroking the killer whale's head. Willy swam out a few feet from the dock and whirled around in the water. "Hey! You remember the old tricks!" Jesse laughed. "You always did know how to cheer me up!"

Out in the distance, Jesse heard a whale song. "That's your mom calling, isn't it?" he said.

Willy rolled on to his side and used his fin to wave goodbye. He was off to join his family for the night. Jesse smiled. Willy *did* remember!

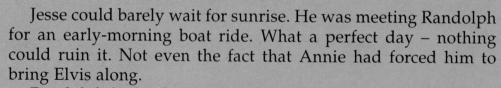

Jesse could barely wait for sunrise. He was meeting Randolph for an early-morning boat ride. What a perfect day – nothing could ruin it. Not even the fact that Annie had forced him to bring Elvis along.

Randolph had a few things to do before he could take Jesse out on the boat. That gave Jesse the time to introduce Willy to Randolph's god-daughter, Nadine. And Jesse definitely didn't want Elvis tagging along.

Elvis was angry with Jesse. He snatched the harmonica from Jesse's jacket and ran to the dock. Elvis blew into the harmonica. It made a loud squawking sound – nothing like the pretty music Jesse played. Still, the sound was nice enough to attract Willy's younger brother, Littlespot. The young orca burst out of the water and started chattering. He wanted to be friends.

That night while everyone slept, an oil tanker called the *Dakar*
pushed its way through the water. The ship was old and in bad
condition. It was no match for the strong ocean currents. All at
once alarm bells blared across the ship.

"We're losing engine pressure," one of the engineers called to
the ship's captain.

The tanker was drifting out of control. Suddenly the *Dakar*
struck the rocks. Thick, gooey oil began to leak from its hull into
the ocean.

The next morning, Jesse woke early. He was eager to see Willy again. But out in the distance, he heard the mournful sound of crying whales. Elvis heard them, too. Together the brothers headed for the cove.

There, Jesse and Elvis found the saddest sight they'd ever seen. A whale was lying on the shore, gasping for breath.

"It's Willy's sister, Luna!" Jesse exclaimed. "She's beached. Elvis, you've got to go tell Glen."

11

Glen immediately called Randolph with the news. Randolph contacted Dr Kate Haley, one of the best vets in the area. There was no time to waste.

"The oil slick is moving this way," Randolph explained to Jesse. "If Luna doesn't get better fast, she'll be trapped in the cove."

Jesse knew Willy and Littlespot would never leave their sister. If Luna died in the cove, they probably would, too.

Dr Haley and her crew boarded a small boat and tried to pull up near Luna.

"They're going to inject Luna with a needle bigger than my arm," Jesse explained to Glen as the two watched from the shore.

The needle was filled with medicine that might make Luna well again. But Willy didn't know that. He didn't realize that Dr Haley was a good doctor. He only remembered the nasty doctors back at the amusement park. The orca was determined to keep his sister away from *any* vet.

Suddenly Willy appeared behind Dr Haley's boat. The mighty whale used all of his strength to push the boat away from his sister. The boat rocked dangerously back and forth.

As Willy swam away he gave Dr Haley a look that said "Don't mess with me!"

Dr Haley wasn't angry. She had great respect for killer whales. Still, she *was* worried that Willy would keep her from helping Luna.

"He thinks he's protecting Luna," Dr Haley explained to Jesse. "In fact, by keeping us from helping her, he's killing her. You're his only friend. You can help him. You can save Luna."

Jesse couldn't say no. He turned to Mr Milner, a man who worked for the oil company. "I'll convince Willy to let us help Luna," he said. "But you have to promise to get Willy, Luna and Littlespot back to their mother."

Mr Milner had no choice. If Luna died, everyone would hate his oil company. He would lose his job. "I promise," he said.

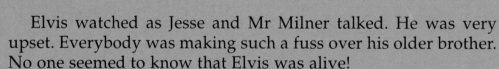

Elvis watched as Jesse and Mr Milner talked. He was very upset. Everybody was making such a fuss over his older brother. No one seemed to know that Elvis was alive!

"I want to help," Elvis told Annie.

"The whales need all the help they can get." Annie smiled. "Everybody has to pitch in."

Annie promised to let Elvis help save Luna. She even did a spit-shake on it!

Jesse was more than a little nervous as he got ready. Willy had been acting so strangely. What if he didn't remember his old tricks?

Jesse played his harmonica and waited for Willy to come.

"Hey, boy, it's me," Jesse said gently. "I'm not going to hurt you. This is Doctor Haley. She's going to help Luna."

17

"We need to get Luna to raise her fluke," Dr Haley explained to Jesse.

Jesse looked Willy in the eye. "You have to show Luna what to do," he said. "If *you* do it, she will."

Jesse gave Willy the signal. Willy waited an instant and then raised his fluke, Jesse watched with relief as Luna slowly copied her brother.

Kate took out the needle and gave Luna her shot.

"Thanks, Willy." Jesse smiled. "You saved your sister's life."

But Luna was still sick. Dr Haley's medicine wasn't helping. It was time for Randolph to try a cure of his own.

Together Randolph and Jesse went into the woods to search for a skookum root and some herbs. Randolph ground them into a paste. Then he and Jesse went out to the cove and rubbed some of the paste on to Luna's tongue.

"We'll have to wait and see if the spirits are with us," Jesse said.

"The spirits are always with us," Randolph answered. "It's luck we need to be with us tonight."

The next morning, Willy and Littlespot were swimming in circles around the cove. There, swimming behind them was Luna! The skookum had worked!

But the whales were not safe yet. They had to leave the cove within the next few hours. Any later and they would be swimming straight into an oil slick.

"This is it, Willy," Jesse told his friend. "You've got to get out of here – now. You've got to make Luna leave."

But Luna was still too weak to leave. So the whales stayed in the cove.

"They've given the order to boom off the cove, seal it completely to keep out the oil and protect the whales," Randolph told Jesse.

"If they're trapped in the cove, they'll never get back to J-Pod – their family!" Jesse cried out.

Back at the camp, Elvis felt very angry. Annie had promised he could help save the whales. But, once again, it was his big brother, Jesse, who had gone to their rescue. Elvis didn't feel very loved – or needed. He ran away.

Running away made Elvis hungry. He went to a café near the ferry terminal and ordered coffee and doughnuts. While he was eating he overheard a *very* interesting conversation!

"A million dollars for each of the young ones and two million for the older brother," the first man said.

"Just so long as it looks like we have the whales' best interests at heart," the second man said.

Elvis knew that voice – it was Mr Milner from the oil company!

"While they're getting nice and healthy, there's no reason people shouldn't pay to see them," the first man laughed.

Finally, Elvis could do something to save the whales.

Elvis raced back to the campsite.

"Where have *you* been?" Jesse asked his younger brother.

"I'll tell you, but you have to trust me," Elvis answered.

"Why should I trust *you*?"

Elvis looked his brother straight in the eye. "Because nobody ever has," he said simply.

Something in Elvis's face made Jesse listen to what his brother had to say.

Jesse, Nadine and Elvis stormed over to the pier.

"You're a liar!" Jesse screamed at Mr Milner. "You're not trying to help these whales. You're selling them to the aquarium! You're not going to get away with it!"

Jesse looked on with horror as Milner's men trapped Littlespot in a large net. Luckily, Willy came to his brother's rescue. He used his nose to flip the boat over and set Littlespot free.

25

Jesse knew the trappers would come back and try again. Willy's family needed his help. The kids leapt into Glen's small motorboat – the *Little Dipper*.

"Let's get out of here!" Elvis cried. Jesse nodded. He steered the *Little Dipper* straight to Willy.

"We're getting out of here. OK?" Jesse called out. "Here's one from the old days." Jesse signalled for Willy to jump.

Willy dived underwater. In a few seconds he burst into the air. The mighty orca twisted his body and crashed down into the ocean with a force so strong the trappers' nets collapsed beneath him.

Willy swam back towards the cove. He pushed at Luna with his snout. But he was not strong enough to move her. Littlespot swam over to help. Together the brothers forced Luna out of the cove and on her way to safety.

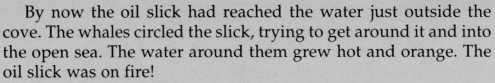

By now the oil slick had reached the water just outside the cove. The whales circled the slick, trying to get around it and into the open sea. The water around them grew hot and orange. The oil slick was on fire!

"Jesse! We have to go back!" Nadine shouted.

But Jesse didn't budge. "I have to make sure they get around the oil."

The smoke was getting thicker and thicker.

"Hey, you guys," Elvis said, "I see something in the water."

"What, like fish?" Nadine asked.

"No. More like . . . rocks!"

Suddenly, Jesse felt a huge thud! The boat slammed into the rocks. Water poured in around his feet. The *Little Dipper* was sinking!

Elvis was really scared. "If you get me out of this, I'll never touch your stuff, or cross the line, or say bad things about you ever again," he promised Jesse.

In the distance the kids heard the whirring of helicopter blades. Before long, the helicopter lowered itself over the *Little Dipper*. A rescue worker leaned out and lowered a harness.

"I'm scared," Elvis said as Jesse helped him into the harness.

"Don't worry, kid," Jesse said, guiding Elvis up towards the helicopter.

Nadine scrambled into the harness next.

It seemed like forever before the harness came back for Jesse. The smoke had become so thick the rescue workers could barely see him. Jesse reached up and grabbed the cable that was holding the rescue harness. But his hands were slippery from the oil. Jesse fell from the harness and landed in the sea – right in the middle of a ring of fire! Nobody could help him. Nobody, that is, except Willy!

The great whale swam to Jesse. Jesse jumped on his friend's back and held his nose. Together they glided beneath the flames.

Jesse gasped for breath as Annie and Glen helped him out of the water and safely on to Randolph's boat.

"You saved his life, Willy," Annie said gratefully.

"I love you, Willy," Jesse added. In the distance he could hear Willy's mother calling him home. Tears welled in Jesse's eyes. He gave Willy the signal to go. Willy belonged with his family.

As Willy swam off, Jesse looked at Elvis. Elvis belonged with *his* family – with Jesse. He walked over and gave his brother a hug.

Jesse grinned. It was pretty wonderful having a family.